Let the Celebrations
B E G I N !

Written by

Margaret Wild

Illustrated by

Julie Vivas

ORCHARD BOOKS · NEW YORK

Orchard Books, A division of Franklin Watts, Inc., 387 Park Avenue South, New York, NY 10016

Printed in Hong Kong   10 9 8 7 6 5 4 3 2 1

Library of Congress Cataloging-in-Publication Data
Wild, Margaret, 1948–   . Let the celebrations begin! / written by Margaret Wild: illustrated by Julie
Vivas.—1st American ed.   p.   cm. Summary: A child, who remembers life at home before life in a
concentration camp, makes toys with the women to give to the other children at the very special party they
are going to have when the soldiers arrive to liberate the camp.
ISBN 0-531-05937-5.   ISBN 0-531-08537-6. (lib. bdg.)
[1. Concentration camps—Fiction. 2. Jews—Fiction.]   I. Vivas, Julie, 1947–   , ill.   II. Title.
PZ7.W64574Le   1991   [E]—de20   90-21606

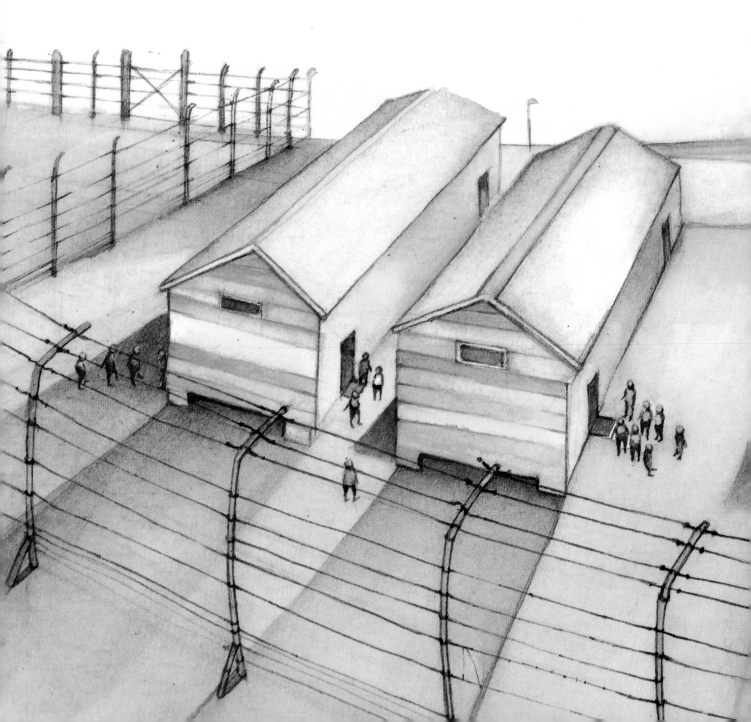

A small collection of stuffed toys has been preserved that were made by Polish women in Belsen for the first children's party held after the liberation.

From *Antique Toys and their Background* by Gwen White
(B. T. Batsford Ltd, London, 1971).

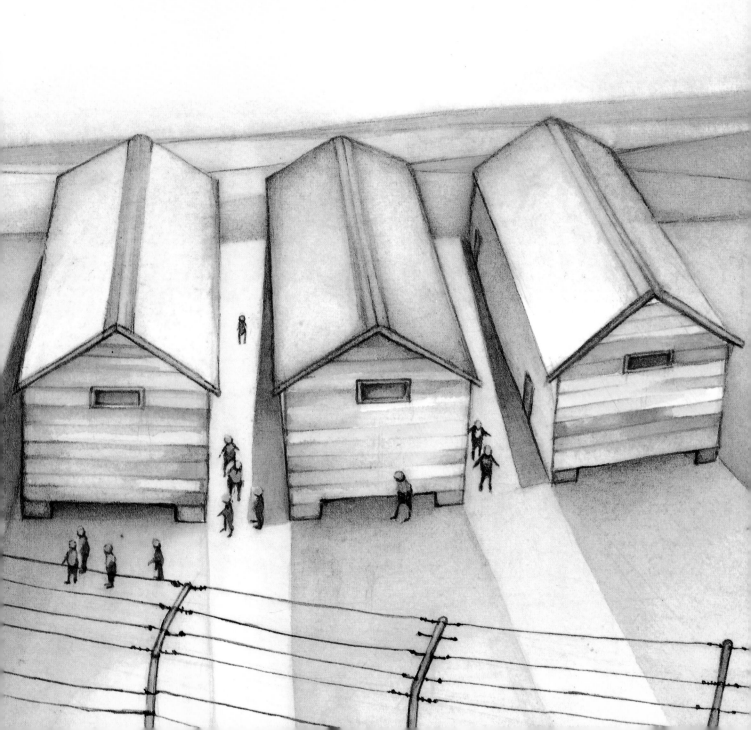

We are planning a party, a very special party, the women and I.

My name is Miriam, and this is where I live. Hut 18, bed 22.

This is my best friend, Sarah, and this is David. He is only
four. See him there in the corner with his mama's old
black shawl. See his hungry eyes and his legs. His legs!
The chickens running in our yard were fatter.

Chickens! It is years since I chewed on a chicken leg.
Back then, I didn't like the skin or fat. Now I would
gobble it all up—skin, fat and bones. I would lick the
plate and pull the wishbone and make sure David had
second helpings, third helpings, fourth helpings
of everything!

Sarah and David think they have always lived here. They think this is their home. But I still remember. I remember Mama and Papa and my very own bedroom and my very own bed and, in the corner, my very own toys.

Sarah and David say to me, "Tell us again, Miriam, tell us about your teddy bear with the squeak in the middle. Tell us about your doll that has eyes that blink. Tell us about your soft pink elephant that sits on the windowsill, and the owl that swings from the ceiling."

So I tell them. Sarah stares at me, and David hugs his mama's old black shawl,

and I run away to be on my own, because I know Sarah and David want a toy more than anything else in the world. And in this place there are no toys.

That is why we are planning a party, a very special party, the women and I. When the soldiers come to set us free—and they are coming soon, everyone says so!—they will open the gates. And for dinner we will cook chickens—chickens for everyone!—and each child in the hut will get a toy. A toy of their own.

We are making the toys now, the women and I. We are collecting bits and pieces. Scraps of material, rags, tiny strands of thread, wool, anything. And we shall make toys—incredible toys!—the women and I.

Old Jacoba says we are mad. "Why do you worry about toys?" she scolds. "We are starving, *dummkopfs*. It is food we need, not your foolish toys."

But we laugh at her, the women and I. And we go on begging buttons and torn pockets, because there is nothing we can do about the food. There *is* no food. But we can make toys. And we shall. In the end, old Jacoba gives us the back of her sweater and goes off grumbling that it will be our fault if she gets rheumatism in her back this winter.

But we shrug and smile because we know we won't still be
in the camp this winter. The soldiers are coming soon—
everyone says so!—and we must be ready, the women
and I, for our party, our very special party.

We are cutting and sewing, all of us, every night while the guards sleep. Even old Jacoba is helping. She has given us the right sleeve of her sweater, and she says it will be our fault—oh yes!—if she gets rheumatism in her right arm this winter.

But still we don't have enough material! So now we are cutting up our own clothes. My skirt is getting shorter and shorter. David is puzzled. He thinks my legs are growing longer and longer, remarkably fast.

Sarah scowls. She knows we have a secret, the women and I, and she says she hates me, she will never speak to me again. But I can't tell her, not yet, not until I have finished making her an elephant that will one day sit on the windowsill of her new home. . . .

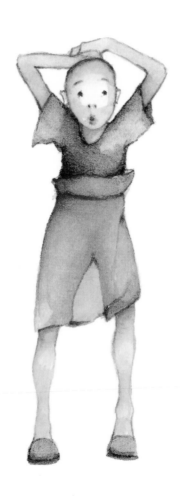

They are here! Everyone, everyone, the soldiers are here!
See their guns and their tanks and the big gates
swinging open!

David peeps at the soldiers through his mama's old black shawl, and the soldiers stare back at us, oh, so strangely, making soft noises in their throats. They seem afraid to touch us—it's as if they think we might break. Then old Jacoba shuffles forward and demands a cooked chicken— all to herself!—and the soldiers laugh and one of them swings David up onto his shoulders.

That night at our party, our very special party, the women and I bring out the toys.

David wraps up his precious owl in his mama's old black shawl.

Sarah hugs her funny patchwork elephant and vows to keep it always on her windowsill.

And old Jacoba tells everyone, very loudly, that she donated her whole sweater—yes!—the back of it, the front, and both sleeves, so that these dear children could have toys.

The women and I wink at one another and pass old Jacoba another helping of chicken soup—

and so the celebrations begin!

Suddenly . . . we heard the sound of rolling tanks. We were convinced that the Germans were about to blow up the camp. But then . . . we heard a loud voice say in German: "Hello, hello, you are free! We are British soldiers, and we came to liberate you!"

We ran out of the barracks and saw . . . a British army car with a loudspeaker on top going through the camp and repeating the same message over and over again. Within minutes, hundreds of women stopped the car, screaming, laughing, and crying, and the British soldier was crying with us.

Recollection of Dr. Hadassah Rosensaft, from *The Liberation of the Nazi Concentration Camps 1945: Eyewitness Accounts of the Liberators*, edited by Brewster Chamberlin and Marcia Feldman (United States Holocaust Memorial Council, Washington, DC, 1987).